IN THE NEIGHBORHOOD

Rocio Bonilla

ini Charlesbridge

*To my family. To my friends. To the ones I love.
To those who are by my side and to those
who feel close even while being far away.*

And to Marta, for always being there.

2022 First US edition
English text copyright © 2022 by Charlesbridge;
    translated by Maya Faye Lethem

First published in Spain as *Gràcies. Història d'un veïnat*
© Text and illustrations by Rocio Bonilla, 2021
© First published by Edicions Bromera, 2021 (www.bromera.com)

At the time of publication, all URLs printed in this book were accurate
and active. Charlesbridge and the author are not responsible for the
content or accessibility of any website.

Published by Charlesbridge
9 Galen Street
Watertown, MA 02472
(617) 926-0329
www.charlesbridge.com

Printed in China
(hc) 10 9 8 7 6 5 4 3 2 1

Hand lettering by Rocia Bonilla
Display type set in BlueCentury by Benoit Desprez
Text type set in Neucha by Jovanny Lemonad
Printed by 1010 Printing International Limited
    in Huizhou, Guangdong, China
Production supervision by Jennifer Most Delaney
Designed by Ellie Erhart

Library of Congress Cataloging-in-Publication Data
Names: Bonilla, Rocio, 1970– author, illustrator.
Title: In the neighborhood / Rocio Bonilla.
Other titles: Gràcies. English
Description: Watertown, MA: Charlesbridge, [2022] | Originally published in
    Alzira, Spain, by Edicions Bromera in 2021 under title: Gràcies. | Audience:
    Ages 3–7. | Audience: Grades K–1. | Summary: "Camila the chicken, Mr.
    Martínez the fox, Phillip the mouse, Rodolfo the cat, Matilda the pig, Mrs.
    Paquita the owl, and Pepe the ogre all live on the same street, but nobody
    talks to anybody else. One day a chain reaction begins that turns this
    neighborhood into a true community."—Provided by publisher.
Identifiers: LCCN 2021033299 (print) | LCCN 2021033300 (ebook) |
    ISBN 9781623543600 (hardcover) | ISBN 9781632892478 (ebook)
Subjects: LCSH: Animals—Juvenile fiction. | Neighbors—Juvenile fiction. |
    Helping behavior—Juvenile fiction. | CYAC: Neighbors—Fiction. | Animals—
    Fiction. | LCGFT: Picture books.
Classification: LCC PZ7.1.B6654 Th 2022 (print) | LCC PZ7.1.B6654 (ebook) |
    DDC [E] —dc23
LC record available at https://lccn.loc.gov/2021033299
LC ebook record available at https://lccn.loc.gov/2021033300

Once upon a time there was a neighborhood like so many others. It had houses, streetlights, trees, and neighbors who had never met one another.

Camila lived at number 15. There was always a lot of noise coming out of her house. The neighbors figured she was hard of hearing so she had to turn up the volume on her TV.

But the real reason for all that noise
was that Camila had ten babies who were
ten bundles of energy!

Camila didn't dare to start up a conversation with her neighbor Mr. Martínez. He seemed so serious and so straightlaced. She was convinced he didn't like kids and wouldn't want to have anything to do with her.

Mr. Martínez worked in the city. He was an important lawyer, just like his mother, grandfather, and great-grandfather before him.

But when Mr. Martínez got home from work,
he changed completely.

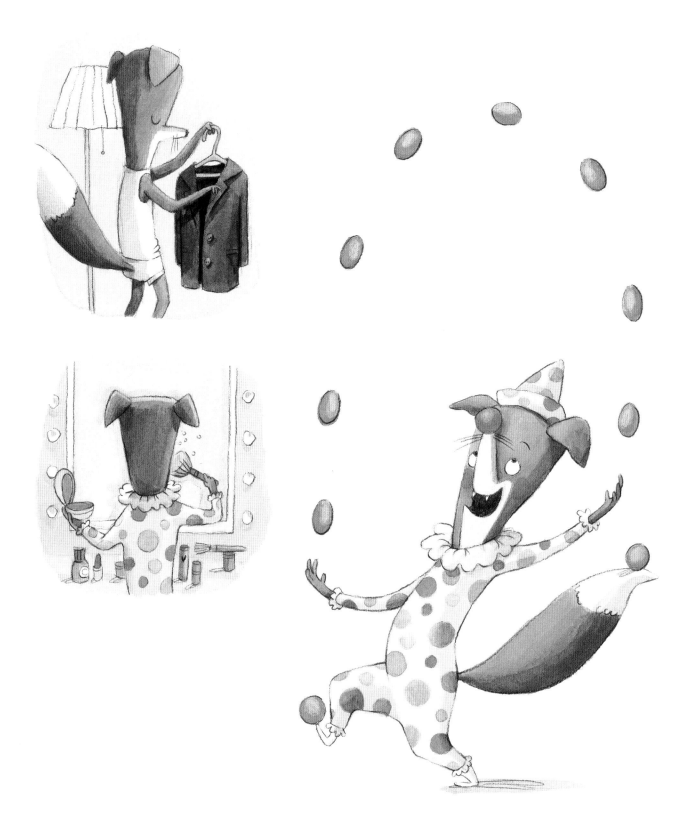

He had a secret hobby: juggling!

"If only I had an audience." He sighed.
His neighbors were a noisy hen and
a huge dragon who didn't seem to have
much of a sense of humor.

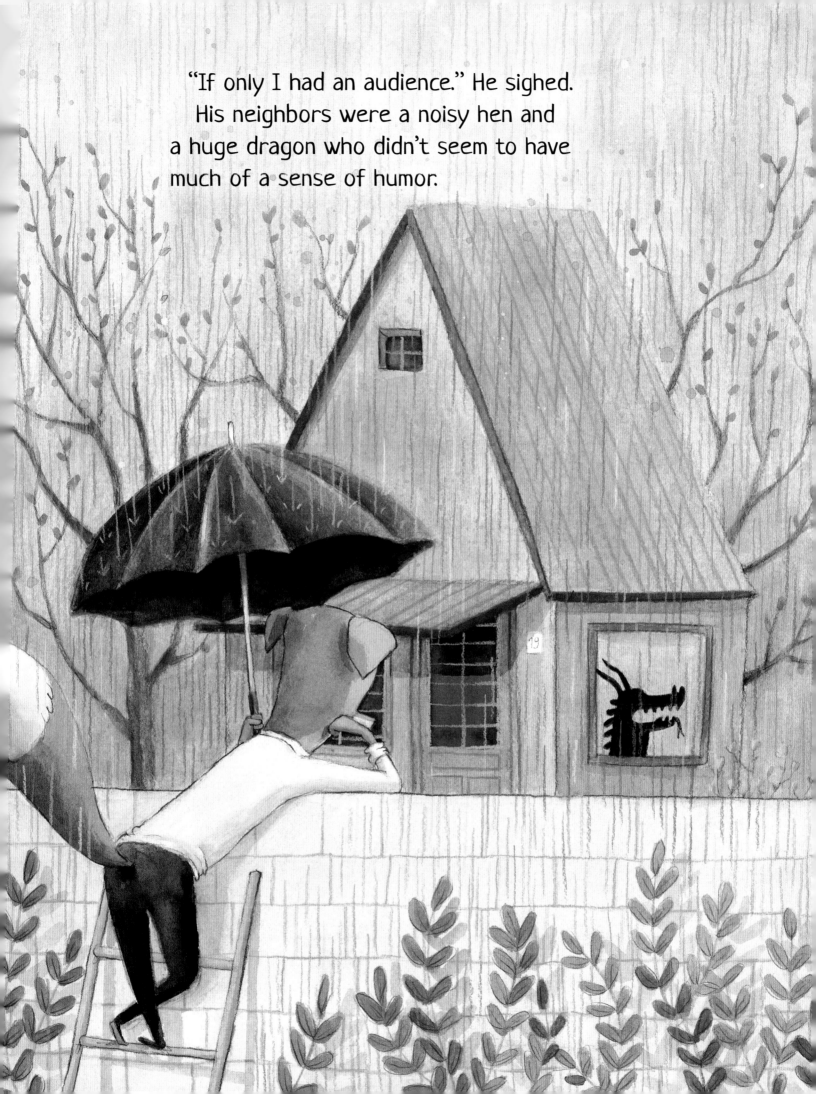

The truth was that there was no
huge dragon living on the street.

Mr. Martínez's neighbor was a little mouse
who lived in fear because a cat had moved in
nearby. We all know what cats like to eat, right?

Phillip the mouse was very creative, and he came up with a clever solution to keep his very dangerous feline neighbor from coming anywhere near him.

What Phillip couldn't possibly imagine was that the cat across the street was vegan, so he never ate mice. Rodolfo the cat loved to play cards, knit pillows, and most of all, lovingly tend his vegetable garden.

Rodolfo was so shy that he'd never even once waved to his neighbor. Would you risk annoying a fierce dragon?

On the corner lived Matilda, a brilliant scientist. She worked all day in her garage, building astonishing inventions.

Matilda spoke only to her robots, because she had no one else to talk to. She figured no one lived next door. That house was always locked up tight.

But someone did live there!

It was just that Mrs. Paquita slept all day, like owls do. Then she spent all night on the internet, reading the news and playing game after game of solitaire.

She didn't even remember to raise her blinds.

Pepe the ogre lived at the top of a beanstalk. No one ever rang his bell, so he never left the house.

He was convinced his neighbors were afraid of him, because ogres have such a bad reputation.

The truth was Pepe was a bookworm who yearned to share his love of reading.

He dreamed about organizing a book club in the neighborhood. Or even better, two: one for books about traveling and another for superhero books, which were his very favorite kind.

Then one fine day something terrible happened.
Mrs. Paquita's internet connection stopped working!
"Oh dear, oh dear! This is horrible," she moaned.

Matilda was shocked to hear her neighbor.
Someone did live next door!
Since Matilda was very handy, she was able
to solve Mrs. Paquita's problem in the blink of
an eye.

The next day Mrs. Paquita realized that she needed one more egg for her cake recipe. She rang her neighbor's doorbell for the first time ever.

Pepe the ogre was very pleased to see she wasn't afraid of him, and he ran down to have tea and cake.

Camila looked out her window and was surprised to see three neighbors eating cake together. That made her think she should try knocking on Mr. Martínez's door.

She found out that he wasn't so straightlaced after all.

Rodolfo the cat got a big surprise when he decided to put aside his fear and shyness to go visit his dragon neighbor for the very first time.

Soon everyone knew one another. They became friends. The neighborhood was now something different—a community.

And everybody was happier.